-2

CHRISTINA'S CAROL

FEATURING THE CLASSIC CHRISTMAS CAROL "IN THE BLEAK MIDWINTER" BY CHRISTINA ROSSETTI

ILLUSTRATIONS BY

 TOMIE dePAOLA ♡

SIMON & SCHUSTER BOOKS FOR YOUNG READERS

NEW YORK   LONDON   TORONTO   SYDNEY   NEW DELHI

In the bleak midwinter
Frosty wind made moan;
Earth stood hard as iron,
Water like a stone;

Snow had fallen, snow on snow,
Snow on snow,
In the bleak midwinter
Long ago.

Our God, heaven cannot hold Him
Nor earth sustain,

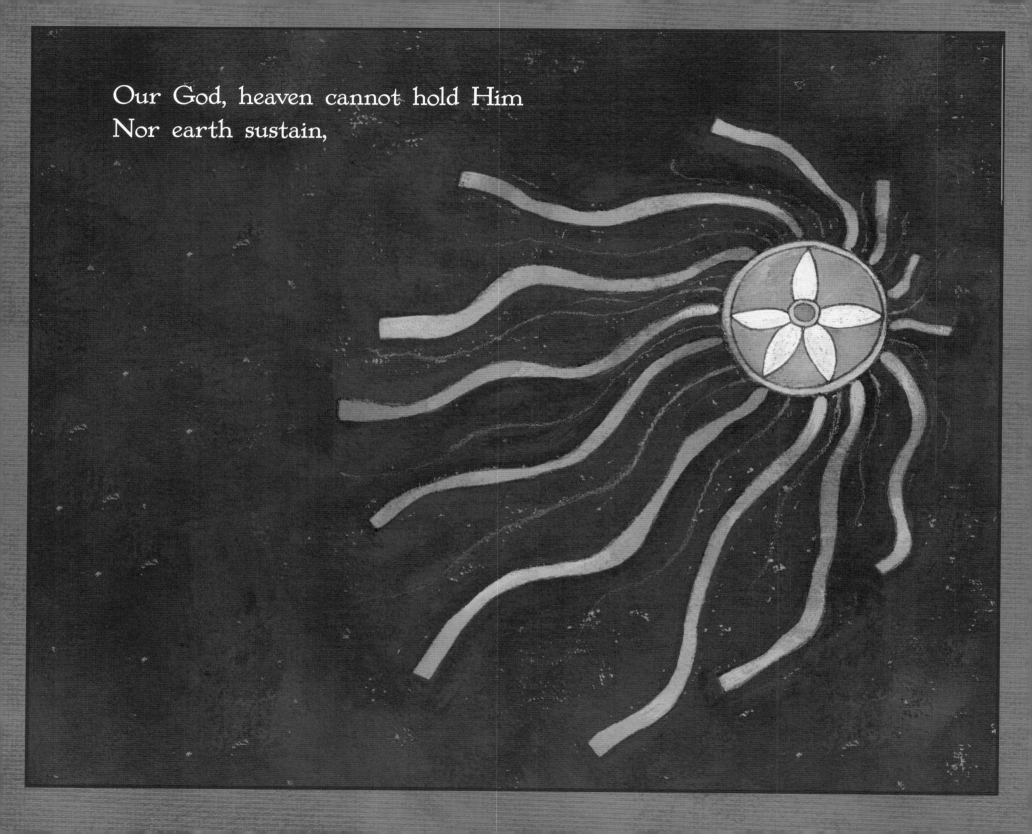

Heaven and earth shall flee away
When He comes to reign:

In the bleak midwinter
A stable-place sufficed

The Lord God Almighty—
Jesus Christ.

Enough for Him, whom cherubim
Worship night and day,

A breastful of milk
And a mangerful of hay;

Enough for Him, whom angels
Fall down before,

The ox and ass and camel
Which adore.

Angels and archangels
May have gathered there,
Cherubim and seraphim
Thronged the air;

But only His mother
In her maiden bliss

Worshipped the Beloved
With a kiss.

What can I give Him,
Poor as I am?

If I were a shepherd
I would bring a lamb;

If I were a Wise Man
I would do my part;

Yet what I can I give Him:

Give my heart.

SIMON & SCHUSTER BOOKS FOR YOUNG READERS
An imprint of Simon & Schuster Children's Publishing Division
1230 Avenue of the Americas, New York, New York 10020
© 2021 by the Estate of Tomie dePaola
Text adapted from "In the Bleak Midwinter" by Christina Rossetti
Book design by Laurent Linn © 2021 by Simon & Schuster, Inc.
All rights reserved, including the right of reproduction in whole or in part in any form.
SIMON & SCHUSTER BOOKS FOR YOUNG READERS and related marks are trademarks of Simon & Schuster, Inc.
For information about special discounts for bulk purchases,
please contact Simon & Schuster Special Sales at 1-866-506-1949 or business@simonandschuster.com.
The Simon & Schuster Speakers Bureau can bring authors to your live event. For more information or to book an event,
contact the Simon & Schuster Speakers Bureau at 1-866-248-3049 or visit our website at www.simonspeakers.com.
The text for this book was set in Colwell.
Manufactured in China
0621 SCP
First Edition
2 4 6 8 10 9 7 5 3 1
Library of Congress Cataloging-in-Publication Data
Names: Rossetti, Christina Georgina, 1830–1894, author. | De Paola, Tomie, 1934–2020, illustrator.
Title: Christina's carol / Tomie dePaola.
Description: First edition. | New York : Simon & Schuster Books for Young Readers, [2021] | Audience: Ages 4–8. | Audience: Grades K–1. |
Summary: Presents an illustrated version of the Christmas carol written by English poet Christina Rossetti.
Identifiers: LCCN 2019035925 | ISBN 9781534418486 (hardcover) | ISBN 9781534418493 (ebook)
Subjects: LCSH: Carols, English—Texts. | CYAC: Carols. | Christmas music.
Classification: LCC PZ8.3.R744 Ch 2020 | DDC 782.42 [E]—dc23
LC record available at https://lccn.loc.gov/2019035925

ILLUSTRATION CREDITS

pp. 10, 27, and jacket back panel: *The Story of the Three Wise Kings*. Copyright © 1983 by Tomie dePaola.
Published by Simon & Schuster Books for Young Readers.

pp. 11, 14 (right), 19 (bottom), 20, 21 (top left and top right), and 32: from the personal collection of Tomie dePaola, copyright © 2021 by Whitebird, Inc.

pp. 12, 24 (bottom), 28, and jacket front flap: *The First Christmas: A Festive Pop-Up Book*. Copyright © 1984 by Tomie dePaola.
Used by permission of G.P. Putnam's Sons Books for Young Readers, an imprint of Penguin Young Readers Group, a division of Penguin Random House. All rights reserved.

pp. 13 (both), 14 (left), 15, 16 (all), 17-18, 19 (top), 21 (bottom), 25, 29, and jacket front panel (bottom left and right): *Tomie dePaola's Book of Christmas Carols*.
Copyright © 1987 by Tomie dePaola. Published by G.P. Putnam's Sons, a division of Penguin Random House.

pp. 22-23: *Merry Christmas, Strega Nona*. Copyright © 1991 by Tomie dePaola.
Published by Houghton Mifflin Harcourt Books for Young Readers.

p. 26: *The Legend of Old Befana*. Copyright © 1980 by Tomie dePaola.
Published by Simon & Schuster Books for Young Readers.

p. 31: *Christmas Remembered*. Copyright © 2006 by Tomie dePaola. Published by G.P. Putnam's Sons, a division of Penguin Random House.